Pedro's Journal

Pedro's Journal

A Voyage with Christopher Columbus
August 3, 1492–February 14, 1493

PAM CONRAD

Inside illustrations by Peter Koeppen

SCHOLASTIC INC.
New York Toronto London Auckland Sydney

With grateful acknowledgment
to naval architect Thomas C. Gillmer
for authenticating Pedro's drawings. — P.K.

ISBN 0-590-29136-X (meets NASTA specifications)

2 3 4 5 6 7 8 9 10   40   00 99 98 97 96 95 94

Printed in the U.S.A.

First Scholastic printing, September 1992

For Ralph Fatturuse
who encouraged me to jump off the side
of the Sarah Moon —P.C.

Pedro's
Journal

August 3

The ship's roster of the *Santa María* has me down as Pedro de Salcedo, ship's boy. And the captain of this ship, who calls himself "Captain General of the Ocean Sea," has hired me not for my great love of the sea, nor for my seamanship, but because I have been taught to read and write, and he thinks it will be useful to have me along.

Last night when I boarded the *Santa María* with forty others and made ready to begin this uncertain journey to India, I saw my mother standing alone on the dock wrapped in her black shawl. She lifted her hand to wave, and I turned away quickly. I have never been away from our home. I have never been on a ship as great as this one. I dedicate this journal, this parcel of letters and drawings, to my dear mother, who has lost so much and who I pray will not lose me as well—me, her young boy whom she calls *Pedro de mi corazón,* Pedro of my heart.

We are a fleet of three ships, the *Niña* and *Pinta* with us, and this morning in the darkness, with no one watching or waving good-bye, we left the harbor at Palos and headed out for the sandbar on the Saltes River. There we waited for tide and wind and then made way for the Canary Islands. We are to be the first ships ever to run a course west to the Indies, Marco Polo's land where palaces are built of gold, where mandarins wear silk brocade and pearls are the size of ripened grapes.

A couple of the men are seasick and are already mumbling that we will never see this India our Captain General is so certain he will find. Me, I have no knowledge of maps or charts or distant journeys. I am only a ship's boy. There are three of us, and I am beginning to suspect that we will do all the work no one wants to do. But already the Captain favors me and has called upon me to write and to copy

certain of his writings. I believe he is testing me and will find I am capable and write a good hand.

The Captain told me he was pleased to see my stomach is as strong as my handwriting and has encouraged me to sketch some of the things I see around me. Perhaps I am a natural seaman, although I admit that looking over the side of this creaking ship into the swelling water can fill me with terror.

August 7

God, give us good days, good voyage,
good passage to the ship,
sir captain and master and good company,
so let there be, let there be
a good voyage;
Many good days may God grant
your graces,
gentlemen of the afterguard
and gentlemen forward.

My mother would be pleased to know that each morning when the crew gathers on the deck, with the sails and lines rattling and clanking and the winds gusting above us, it is her own dear son who leads the morning prayers. She would also be amused to see the way the Captain says his rosary with such a fury, as if his prayers are orders to be carried out immediately.

I am learning the names and terms of all things to do with sailing and ships. In just a short time—given the Captain's lack of patience and fiery temper—I have learned to pretend that I know what everything means. I nod my head yes to his orders and then I search out someone who can explain what I must do.

Yesterday, after only four days out, the Captain was disturbed because the rudder broke on the *Pinta*. The rudder is the part that goes into the water to steer the ship, so of course we all had to wait.

I went with him to the *Pinta* in our ship's small dinghy to see what was wrong. The ocean tossed and threw us about, and I held onto the sides for dear life while Columbus and Martín Alonso Pinzón, the captain of the *Pinta*, shouted instructions back and forth to each other. We didn't get too close to the *Pinta* for fear of being crushed against her sides, but we were close enough to see what was wrong, and close enough to see that

Martín Alonso was able to rig the broken rudder with rope.

Columbus was pleased for the moment that his captain had come up with an ingenious solution to the problem, and we returned to the *Santa María*. Last night Columbus wrote in his log that he believes it had been done on purpose, that there are men on board the *Pinta* who do not wish to make this journey.

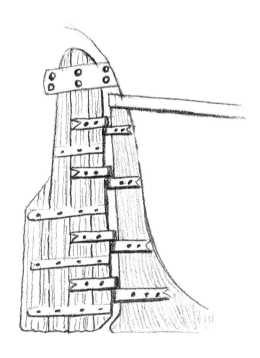

Now those ropes on the rudder have all broken in a hard wind. More repairs must be made, or a replacement ship must be found. There is a brooding silence about the crew, and I am surprised to learn through mumblings and complaints that few of the men want to make this voyage. No one has much faith. And they whisper among themselves of sea monsters and how the sea will come to an abrupt end and we will go toppling off the edge of the world like a log careening over a waterfall.

My Captain seems like a smart man. I cannot believe he would do something so foolish. So I turn away from the men when they speak so, but late at night, when I lie sleeping beneath my covers, sometimes I bolt awake, sure we are falling through space and that we've left the world behind.

August 27

The long voyage lies ahead of us. I learn that when we depart from these Canary Islands we are in uncharted seas. Yet I wonder if we will ever leave. First we wait for a ship to replace the *Pinta*, which not only has a broken rudder but also is leaking, and now it seems there is no replacement and she will have to be repaired. All day long the men row from boat to boat, the boatswain, carpenters, caulkers—experts all—who swear they have solutions to the problem. There is much hammering and shouting as we toss about, straining our anchor lines and the nerves of the waiting sailors.

Then when it seems we are ready to depart on the long trek, Columbus gives the order to change the rigging of the *Niña* from lateen rigging to square rigging, believing she will handle better in the

wind. The sailors all moan. It may be a few more days.

In the heat of noon yesterday some of the men leaped overboard and swam and washed. I want to do this, but not yet. I am too afraid and worry about being swept away from the *Santa María*, away from the hearing of my fellows. They call to me, "Come on, Pedro, leap it! Leap it!" but I am too afraid.

September 3

During my watch it is my job to turn the sandglass exactly as it empties and call out the time. I let the crew know what time it is and remind them all to pray that we are protected on this journey. Then I call them to dinner.

Each morning I wash the slate of the navigator's notes after they've been transcribed into the Captain's formal log, and then I carry this log back to his cabin, where he writes in it alone. He writes each morning about the night before and every night about the day just passed. He draws navigational charts that I do not understand even after studying them. He does not know that I try to learn this. When I hear his step on the wooden stairs from the deck to his cabin, I shut the log and look busy.

On deck I peer into the west, where, it is said, others from the Canary Islands have sworn to see land on clear days. I see nothing. My new friend, Diego García, tells me if we believe these people that there is land there, we must also believe their sightings of sea monsters and mermaids. He says this and laughs, but when I look west and then down into the dark waters that will carry us, I think I can believe anything.

Today we took on fresh supplies. We have used up so much that was to have taken us across the ocean because of the delay with the *Pinta*'s rudder. We have some fruit that we must eat quickly or it

will go bad, wine, molasses, dried meat and salted fish, biscuits. The Captain has written in his log that we have taken on enough supplies to last us twenty-eight days. What will we eat after twenty-eight days if we have not found an Indian port? We cannot then turn around and come home. We will not make it. Oh, dear Mother, I hope you are praying for the speedy return of your only living son.

September 10

Everyone seemed crazy all day. No one is doing his job well. Even the helmsman steered improperly and took us north instead of west. I thought the Captain would string up the whole crew to the mast. "What do you think you are doing?" he shouted. "Steering a ferryboat across the River of Seville?" I've seen him go into white rages and then pace his small cabin saying his Hail Marys.

We finally lost sight of land as we sailed west. Some say it will be a long time before we see it again. If at all. A couple of the men were crying, and the Captain shamed them and then promised them all sorts of riches and fame. He has said that the first man to spot land will receive a reward of 10,000 maravedis.

The men listen to him sullenly, and I see them exchange glances. They don't believe him, and after what I saw this morning, I wonder if they should. I noted that the morning's slate said we made 180 miles, and yet the Captain recorded only 144 in his official log that the men see. I believe he is trying to make the crew believe that we are closer to home than is true.

But 10,000 maravedis! Ah, think of all I could buy for my mother. Even now I can picture a beautiful dress, a rich dress that she could wear to Mass at Easter. I will keep a sharp eye. I will be the first to spot land!

September 13

Good is that which passeth,
Better that which cometh,
Seven is past and eight floweth,
More shall flow if God willeth,
Count and pass makes voyage fast.

Everyone is worried. They say that Christopher Columbus is mad. Last night and this morning a reading was taken of our compass card off the North Star. I don't understand fully, but they are saying the readings were different and off by quite a bit. Some of the crew say that because we are in uncharted and dangerous seas, our compasses will no longer work and we will be lost forever.

The Captain has stated simply and with authority that last night the North Star moved. It is that simple. That is all.

September 17

What strange things we have seen. One day there was a large mast floating in the water. The sailors said it must have belonged to a ship weighing at least 120 tons. Where is that ship now? What has happened to it? And where are we? What are these waters that devour huge ships and spit out the broken pieces?

Then, something else. I was not there to see it, for it was not my watch, but the other night some of the crew saw a falling star crash into the water. There were whispers that this is a bad omen, forebodes ill for our journey, but the Captain told stories all day of other meteorites he's seen during his sailing career and how they have all portended great blessings and grace. Everyone seemed comforted. He says these things to the crew, yet in his journal he writes that he has never had one fall so close to his ship before. . . .

The weather is lovely right now, so that helps everyone's state of mind. There are mild breezes and light rain showers now and then, and the crew is excited that we are sailing through tremendous patches of yellow-green seaweed. It must mean we are near land. Maybe the Captain is right after all. We saw a school of porpoises swimming beside us, and someone harpooned one. I felt sad to see it die and leave its small family, but then we saw a live crab on the seaweed, a sure sign we are approaching land. The cook boiled up the tiny crab, and it was served to the Captain amidst much laughter and good cheer.

September 18

Last night the wind howled through our shrouds and the ship rolled and lifted like a child tossed in a blanket. I slept not a wink. This morning it is calmer, with the bluest of skies and huge billowing clouds above us, and the ocean becoming flatter and smoother. Later, while taking the log to the Captain's cabin, the Captain and I spotted a tern flying over the ship. He was excited and said land could not be far beyond now. He immediately ordered soundings to be taken to see how deep the ocean is where we are sailing. Even at 200 fathoms, our longest measure, there is nothing. Perhaps there is no bottom. A few are saying the wind will not take us back to Spain. We are entering a place from which we will never return. When I went to see Sancho, my friend and helmsman, early this morning before the Captain came up, he let me hold the tiller and steer a bit. It is harder than it looks, but I did well. Sancho says I may grow to be a captain of my own ship one day and sail all over the world.

September 21

This is the most peculiar thing I have ever seen.
And men on board who are four times my age say it
is the most peculiar thing they have ever seen as
well. The seaweed has grown much worse. We woke
this morning to a meadow of pale green as far as the
eye can see. They pull up stickloads of the odd green
and yellow shoots with air-filled berries that keep
them afloat. There is no way around this covering,
and searching out open seas may take us way off

course, so we continue on, the prow of our ship splitting the field like a farm plow tearing up the earth. One of the men said if the wind stops we are all dead. We will be locked here for all eternity in a mat of thickening weeds. I think not. It almost appears that if that were to happen we could all climb over and walk home across the meadow. I told this to Diego, who laughed at me—me, the boy who won't jump overboard for a swim about to jump overboard for a stroll across seaweed. He said I would sink like a wet boot. And float to the top dripping with weeds.

September 25

We have come to clear waters at last. So clear and so calm that once again I had a chance to swim with the crew. But this time a few of the men threatened to toss me over, claiming that was the only way to learn, but luckily Diego threatened to teach a lesson to whoever tried such a thing. He went ahead of me and called to me as I sat for a long while on the gunwale. Out in the sun with my shirt off, I was surprised to see how brown my hands had gotten from the wrist down.

"Leap, Pedro! I am here," Diego called.

"I'm frightened," I answered, and the others laughed, trying to splash me from the water. The Captain was behind me, his arms crossed, his face serious.

"Can you swim, sir?" I asked him.

"Like a porpoise," he answered. "And I have come to observe over the years that those who take easily to the written word—scribes, readers—they are the best swimmers."

It was what I needed. I looked down into the calm ocean. And at the men who couldn't read and yet were floating before me like so many corks. I thought of my letters, my journal, the Captain's heavy log, and, keeping my eyes on Diego, I slid myself to the very edge and went over. But I am ashamed to say I was not sea-wet within the next instant. I was suddenly dangling over the side by a cleat that had hooked onto my pants. Screaming and kicking, I hung above the water and the crew's hooting. Even Diego—I could hear him laughing. Until suddenly I felt a hand clasp my arm and felt my pants eased off the cleat. I was free.

I flew straight down like a diving bird, and once smacking the cold, wet surface, I went down farther and farther. I feared I would never come up, just continue down away from Diego and my Captain and the *Santa María*. But soon I was emerging and there were friends around me, their laughing faces transformed by the hair laid flat and wet against their heads. A couple took hold of me, and I held on for dear life. Little by little they taught me to tread water, to dive below and open my eyes to an incredible light of green. I guess the Captain was right. I didn't want to go back on board. I dove deeper and deeper, paddling like mad to catch my breath and find Diego. But after a while we all climbed back up on board. I was shivering, and Sancho told everyone to look at my blue lips. I am sorry I waited so long to try this.

September 26

Amen and God give us a good night
and good sailing;
May the ship make a good passage,
Sir captain and good company.

Last night nearing sunset, we were sailing alongside the *Pinta,* and our Captain and the

Pinta's captain were calling back and forth, discussing the use of a certain chart. The sky was spectacular, striped with colors and softness, and all about us the sea was a quiet, slow river. Suddenly a cry went up on the *Pinta* that stunned us all.

"Land! Land, sir! I claim the reward! 10,000 maravedis are mine!"

An incredible sight! On all three ships the men scrambled up the rigging, higher and higher, wherever they could get a grip with their toes and their hands. Even I clambered as high as I could

along the mast, which was not too high but high enough to see in the distance what appeared to be a tall mountain, clear and sharp like ice chiseled against the sky. We shielded our eyes against the setting sun, and in the soft pink air a great triple shout of joy went up across the small stretch of our sea. When I looked down at the deck, I saw the Captain on his knees in prayer.

I am sorry, however, to report this morning that after sailing all night in the southwesterly direction of that chiseled mountain, we have found nothing. Not even a sandbar. It had just been a squall cloud on the horizon at sunset. Nothing more. Nothing less.

Everyone is quiet. There is still a chance for each of us to win the reward.

September 30

The Captain believes land must be very near. We have seen terns regularly these last few days, and petrels, not to mention frigate birds and dorados, and flying fish that land right on our decks. But Columbus is the only one who takes these things as encouraging.

There has been very little wind, and what there is comes at our stern, pushing us along very slowly. The men are bored and restless, with not much to do. They are cleaning and trolling for fish, and cleaning, and checking gear, fishing, cleaning, and always, constantly scanning the western horizon for their pile of 10,000 maravedis.

The Captain is muttering to himself a lot these days. I followed him from the forecastle to the cabin with his log, and to one group of men he said that if there were a mutiny, that if it had occurred to them to return to Spain without him, they would all be hanged. The men stared at him as blank as cows. To the next group of men he promised gold nuggets and gold blankets, gold rings and gold bowls. He boasted to them that we have surpassed the record: we have been out of sight of land now for three weeks. I do not think that particular bit of information was comforting to the men. They only stare at him and say nothing in his presence.

October 5

Last night I could not sleep. All I could think about was my mother and what would happen to her if I were never to return, if the *Santa María* just kept sailing westward forever, trapped in this endless sea that goes nowhere. How would she ever know what became of me? Would she think me dead? Would she look for me forever and then die herself, only for me to return years later and find her gone? I feared in the loneliness of my snug corner that I might begin to cry and wake someone. So, wrapping my blanket about my shoulders, I made my way to the deck for some air.

The night watch—were it not for having to sleep during the day—is my favorite. There is a peace and stillness that surrounds our ship that is like nothing else. And this one night I will remember for the rest of my life, if that be long or short. There was a full brilliant moon in the sky lighting our way. In a path held out before us, the sea was lit, and the prow of our ship headed towards it. Always towards it. The only sounds were the whoosh of the wind in the sails and the gentle churnings of our wake, sounds that are as familiar to me now as my own breath and heartbeat.

I thought of my mother and knew the moon lit my face like a giant lantern. I looked up into the sky and tried to remember her face, and as I did three birds flew across the face of the moon and I knew that in Spain, in the mountains, she was looking at the same moon.

October 7

On deck, on deck,
Mr. Mariners of the right side,
On deck in good time,
you of Mr. Pilot's watch,
For it's already time.
Shake a leg!

We have picked up considerable speed and distance this first week in October, but there is only one thing we are certain of: we grow farther and farther from Spain. The Captain writes in his journal, wondering if somehow we have missed Japan. We have gone much more than the expected 750 leagues. Surely, if this is so, we are on our way to China now and will soon spot the mainland.

This morning there was another false cry of "Land!" This time from the *Niña*. The Captain was upset with her, that she had sailed on ahead, probably to see land first. He wants to be first, to be in the lead. But at sunrise there was the cry, followed by gunfire to signal land and also the sending up of a flag. We followed the *Niña* all day at top speeds to the western point, only to discover nothing. By sunset no land had risen from the sea, and the Captain shouted that from now on whoever gave a false sighting of land would be disqualified from any future rewards.

As he shouted at the men, a whole flock of birds flew over his head, and he grew quiet and watched them. We all watched them disappear into the southwest. "Alter course," Columbus said, suddenly calm and assured. "West-southwest. We'll follow them to their nests."

October 8

Last night, Sancho let me steer some more by myself. He lets me do this only when no one is around and when conditions are very gentle. I see how it takes all his strength to keep the ship on course when the winds and waves toss us about. But when things are quiet and he lets me take the tiller, Sancho lies on the floor beside me and dozes. If I hear a footstep, or if the wind begins to howl, I kick him and he is instantly awake and in charge. But when I am at the tiller and I feel the pressure of the ocean weighing on the ease of the tiller, and I can hear Sancho snoring away, then I am a Captain

myself, a Captain of the Newly Discovered Seas, Explorer, Adventurer, Granter of Maravedis, and I am returning home with my ship stocked to overflowing with cargo. There are bolts of cloth as fine as a new goat's belly, and spices that fill the hold with fine aromas, and gold, gold that shines so brightly that no candles or lanterns are needed below. And all my men respect and revere me, and kings and queens will meet me at the ports.

This is what I think as I keep my eye on the star that Sancho tells me to steer to. But I tell no one, not even Sancho or Diego, of my imaginings, for then they would think there are two crazy sailors on board: me and Columbus.

October 10

This has been the worst day of all for the Captain. I am certain of this. We have doubled all previous records of days and leagues at sea, and we've gone way past the point where he originally said we would find land. There is nothing out here. Surely we are lost. And everyone is certain now as well.

This morning the men responded slowly to orders, scowling and slamming down their tools and lines. They whispered in pairs and small groups on deck and below. The air was thick with mutiny and betrayal, until finally everything came to a dead stop. The wind howled through the shrouds, and the men just stood there on deck and did not move aside when Columbus came.

"Enough," one of the men said to his face. "This is enough. Now we turn back."

The other men grumbled their assent and

nodded, their fists clenched, their chests broad. And they remained motionless and unmoved while Columbus paced the deck, telling them how close he figured we must be, that land could be right over the next horizon. He told them again of the fame and fortune that would be theirs if they could only last a little longer. And they laughed at him, the cruel laughter of impatient and defeated men.

"All that aside," he added, "with the fresh easterly wind coming at us and the rising sea, we can't turn a course back to Spain right now. We would stand still in the water."

I looked up at the sails, full and straining, taking us farther and farther from Spain. What if a westerly wind never came? What if we were just blown away forever and ever?

"Let me offer you this," Columbus finally said. "Do me this favor. Stay with me this day and night, and if I don't bring you to land before day, cut off my head, and you shall return."

The men glanced at each other. Some nodded. "One day," they said. "One day, and then we turn around."

"That is all I ask," Columbus said.

Later, when I went down to the cabin with the

log, the Captain's door was bolted shut, and when I knocked he didn't answer, so I sat outside the door with the heavy journal in my lap and waited.

October 11

Through the day, the day that was to have been our last day traveling westward, many things were seen floating in the water, things that stirred everyone's hopes and had the men once again scanning the horizon. We saw birds in flocks, reeds and plants floating in the water, and a small floating board, and even a stick was recovered that had iron workings on it, obviously man-made. Suddenly no one wished to turn around. There was no further word on it.

At sunset, I led the prayers and the men sang the *Salve Regina*. Then the Captain spoke to the seamen from the sterncastle, doubling the night watch and urging everyone to keep a sharp lookout. No one asked about turning back. Then the Captain added a new bonus to his reward of 10,000 maravedis. He added a silk doublet, and some of the men joked with each other. Next the Captain nodded to me, and I sang for the changing of the watch, but my words were lost in the wind that was growing brisker and in the seas that were growing heavier and sounding like breakers all about us. The men dispersed to their watches and their bunks, and the Captain paced the deck. I don't know why, but this night I stayed with him. I stayed still by the gunwale, watching over the side. Once in a while he would stand beside me, silent, looking westward, always westward.

Then, an hour before moonrise, the Captain froze beside me. "Gutierrez!" he called to one of the king's men on board, who came running. He pointed out across the water. "What do you see?"

Gutierrez peered into the west. "I don't see anything," he said. "What? What? What do you see?"

"Can't you see it?" the Captain whispered. "The light? Like a little wax candle rising and falling?"

The man at his side was quiet. I was there beside him, too, straining my own eyes to the dark horizon.

Suddenly another seaman called out across the darkness, "Land! Land!"

"He's already seen it!" I shouted. "My master's already seen it!" And the Captain laughed and tousled my hair.

"Tierra! Tierra!" It was heard all across the water from all three ships.

I am below now in the Captain's cabin writing, while in the light of the rising moon, with our sails silver in the moonlight, we three exploring ships are rolling and plunging through the swells towards land. Tomorrow our feet will touch soil, and I can assure my dear mother in the hills of Spain that no one will get much sleep on board the *Santa María* tonight!

October 12

A lush green island was there in the morning, and our three ships approached it carefully, maneuvering through breakers and a threatening barrier reef. We could see clear down to the reef in the sparkling blue waters as we sailed through. And, ah, it is truly land, truly earth, here so far from Spain. The *Santa María* led the way into the sheltered bay of the island and got a mark of only five fathoms' depth. We anchored there and barely paused to admire the breathtaking beauty. Small boats were prepared, armed, and lowered, and in these some of us went ashore. Out of respect, all waited while Christopher Columbus leaped out of the boat, his feet the first to touch this new land. (I wondered what my mother would say if she knew her son had lost the 10,000 maravedis to the Captain, who claimed it for himself.)

The Captain carried the royal banner of our king

and queen, and as everyone else scrambled out of the boats and secured them in the white sand, he thrust the banner into the earth and then sank down to his knees and said a prayer of thanksgiving for our safe arrival in India. Others dropped to their knees around him. Diego was beside me, and he clapped his hand on my shoulder. I knew he was happy to be on land again. I was, too, although I have been at sea so long that even on land the ground seems to buckle and sway beneath my feet.

The Captain made a solemn ceremony and formally took possession of the land for the king and queen, naming it San Salvador. We all witnessed this, and then little by little we noticed something else—there were people stepping out from the trees, beautiful, strong, naked people, with tanned skin and straight black hair. My mother would have lowered her eyes or looked away, as I have seen her do in our home when someone dresses, but I could not take my eyes off them. Some had boldly painted their bodies or their faces, some only their eyes, some their noses. They were so beautiful and gentle. They walked towards us slowly but without fear, smiling and reaching out their hands.

The sailors watched them in wonder, and when these people came near, the crew gave them coins, little red caps, whatever they had in their pockets. Columbus himself showed one native his sword, and the native, never having seen such an instrument before, slid his fingers along the sharp edge and looked startled at his fingers that dripped blood into the sand.

Everyone was smiling and so friendly. Close up, we could see how clear and gentle their eyes were, how broad and unusual their foreheads. The Captain especially noted and said to one of his men, "See the gold in that one's nose? See how docile they are? They will be easy. We will take six back with us to Spain."

I think at this, too, my mother would have lowered her eyes.

October 16

So much has happened. There is so much to remember and record, and so much I do not think I want to tell my mother. Perhaps I will keep these letters to myself after all. The natives think that we are angels from God. They swim out to us, wave,

throw themselves in the sand, hold their hands and faces to the sky, and sing and call to us. The crew loves it, and no one loves it better than Columbus. He lifts his open palms to them like a priest at mass. I sometimes wonder if he doesn't believe these natives himself just a little bit.

They come right out to the ship in swift dugouts that sit forty men, and sometimes as they approach us the dugout tips, but in minutes they right it and begin bailing it out with hollow gourds. All day long the Indians row out to see us, bringing gifts of cotton thread, shell-tipped spears, and even brightly colored parrots that sit on our shoulders and cry out in human voices. For their trouble we give them more worthless beads, bells, and tastes of honey, which they marvel at.

The six native men Columbus has taken aboard are not very happy. One by one they are escaping, which I cannot help but say I am happy for. One jumped overboard and swam away, and another jumped overboard when a dugout came up alongside us in the darkness. Some of the crew seized another man coming alongside in a dugout and forced him on board. Columbus tried to convince him of our good intentions through sign language and broken words and more gifts of glass beads and junk, and the man rowed back to some people on the shore. They stood talking to each other and pointing at our ship. Columbus smiled and was convinced they know we are from God. Me, I am not so sure they will believe it for much longer.

October 23

I do not like all the parrots that are on board now. Even Diego has taken a liking to one that sits on his shoulder all day and calls out the names of Spanish ports. Fortunately, this is the only parrot that does not try to bite my ear as I pass.

Our days are spent exploring the coast of San Salvador and the nearby islands. Every time we set foot on new land, Columbus drives his staff into the sand and names the place. He is like Adam in the Bible, naming the animals. Actually there are no

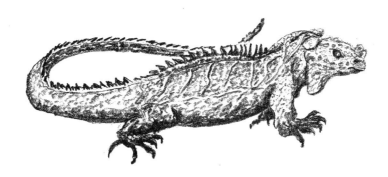

animals here, just fish and birds. And some strange serpents. One day I saw what I thought was a snake, with snakelike skin, and when I drew close, it rose up on feet and walked away. Birds are everywhere, and the water is so clear and blue that when you look down into it you can see the fish swimming through the waters, fish as colorful as the birds.

And the natives will do anything for us, from carrying our water to trading their few possessions for pieces of broken glass. I traded a small bowl for a spear that had a seashell at its tip and carvings down its shaft. I'll take it home to my mother.

Once I was walking with the Captain through a village when we met a man wearing nothing but a string about his waist and a plug in his nose that was clearly made of gold. The Captain stared and stared at it. In signs he asked the man for it, even offering his belt in exchange, but the man waved his hands at us in refusal. I was glad the Captain did not force the matter. As we walked away he whispered to me, "Did you see? There was Japanese writing on that piece of gold. We must be close to Japan."

So in the morning we set sail for Japan.

October 29

The wind was so slight that Columbus put up every sail we had—the main course with her two bonnets, the main topsail, the fore course, spritsail under the bowsprit, lateen mizzen, and even a bonaventure mizzen on the poop, but as we approached a new island at dark, we had to strip to bare poles for fear of sailing wildly into a reef or shoals that are invisible to us.

At dawn we could see the lush palm trees, and when we rowed ashore we saw the large huts where many families lived together. We saw their fishing nets woven from palm threads, and fishhooks and harpoons made from bones. And some of the crew tried something quite bizarre. The natives showed them *tobacos*. Dry leaves are rolled up and lit with a flame, and then the smoke is inhaled into the nostril. While the natives seem to really enjoy doing this, it made some of the crew cough and retch.

That aside, the crew is quite happy. The Indian girls are very pretty and sport freely with them. At sundown prayers they gather with us on the beach and add their voices to our *Ave Maria* even though they don't know the words. Columbus is charmed when they imitate making the sign of the cross. He is sure they will make good subjects for the king.

But where is this Japan? Where are the splendid cities with marble jetties and stone bridges? Where are the temples, and the spices? Where are we?

November 6

While the *Santa María* was beached to have her hull scrubbed, the Captain sent an embassy of us led by Rodrigo into the interior of this island. It is difficult for the natives to understand us and for us to know if they are hearing us correctly. When they were asked about gold and the emperor of China, they pointed inland and offered to lead us there. It was a long, difficult trek through dense jungle and cover. Instead of a city of pavilions and temples, we were taken to a village where there were many friendly people and about fifty large palm huts. These people too thought we were angels from God, and after feeding us and letting us sit in a special chair—a strange carved seat with legs and arms, a tail, and a face—they wanted the women and children to kiss our hands and feet. I did not let them do this to me. I am too young for such honors. Rodrigo is too old for such honors, and if I were to admit the truth, there was no one in our embassy worthy of such adoration. I couldn't wait to get back to the *Santa María.*

When we finally returned she was in the water again but hardly a haven for me from seeing things that make me uncomfortable. While we were gone five more young native men were detained, and word is they will be converted and taken back to Spain as servants.

November 19

I think being lost at sea with no end to our
journey was better than this. If I had only known
this is what awaited us, I would have gladly sailed on
and on through kingdom come, and my mother
would have understood.

Shame fills me like wine in a leather flask, swelling
me from inside and sealing my heart in its darkness.
I remember the summer my mother's goat bore two
tawny kids, and how my mother let them suckle and

grow and kept them about until they were almost as big as their mother. When she finally took them to market, she cried all the way home and wouldn't speak the rest of the night. The next day she said only that it broke her heart to see families torn apart. I laughed at her and said it was only goats, my first shame, but the sound of that nanny's bleating those nights kept me awake and filled me, too, with a sad ache.

I would not laugh at my mother anymore. One day this past week our party had taken on "seven head of women, large and small, and three children." This is the way it is recorded in the Captain's journal. By nightfall a small band of native men rowed out to us and asked to be taken, too. These were the husbands and fathers. Columbus thought they would make good servants and interpreters, so he welcomed them aboard. If goats upset my mother, this would surely tear her apart.

November 25

We are still sailing here and there, searching every island for pieces of gold and signs of Chinese civilization, but so far there is nothing. On one island I was the first to spot the tall pine trees, trees straight enough and strong enough to make a new mizzenmast and lateen yard for the *Niña*. Columbus says this is a splendid island, and with its wonderful trees it can be a future shipyard where seagoing ships will someday be built and sent off.

We see an island that the natives on board tell us is Bohio. They say it is a tremendous island, and that the people there have faces like dogs and a single eye in the center of their foreheads. They tell us that when these people capture prisoners, they eat them. Columbus believes they may be Chinese soldiers.

Then there is some bad news. On the 21st, unexpectedly and for no apparent reason, other than maybe greed and rivalry, the *Pinta* suddenly sailed away. We have not seen her since then. Now we are only two ships.

December 3

We are anchored in a quiet harbor in scattered showers. It has been raining for days without the slightest breeze or gust. Many of the men went ashore to wash their clothes and themselves in the river. Two men wandered into the jungle and returned to tell us they had come upon a village where hanging from a post was a basket with a man's head in it. I don't think I will go looking in any baskets I find.

One day I went ashore with Diego, Columbus, and a native who is working as an interpreter for us. The Captain gave Diego a bag of brass rings, glass beads, and bells and told him to see what trading he could do. Diego agreed, but I could tell he does not like to do this. A group of natives joined us, but these were not so friendly, and they had little to trade. Their eyes were distrustful, and their bodies were painted red, with bundles of feathers and darts hanging from them. When we finished our meager trade, they gathered at the stern of our small boat in the river, and one began making a speech we could not understand. The others began to shout in response. Columbus stood by looking pompous and arrogant as he waited, but the interpreter with us turned pale and began to shake. He told the Captain to go back to the *Santa María* at once, that they were planning to kill us.

I hopped right in the boat to go back, but Diego didn't move and Columbus laughed. He interrupted the village speechmaker and drew his sword from his scabbard. With a gentle smile on his face, he showed him the steel glistening in the sun, sliced clear through a leather strap the speechmaker bore around his neck, and the man's beads tumbled into the sand. Next the Captain had one of his men demonstrate his crossbow. At this the crowd of natives turned and ran into the trees. Our interpreter was still not comforted. He jumped into the boat beside me and, trembling, beckoned us to get aboard and get back to the ship, quickly.

The Captain was slow about it. He talked of how he admired the workmanship of these natives, but

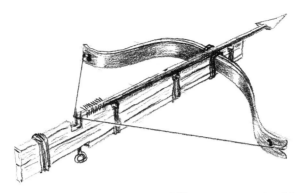

how cowardly they were: "They are so timid, ten of
our men could frighten away thousands of them."
I said nothing. The Captain expects nothing of me.
I just watched silent Diego's back straining and
bulging in rhythm as he helped row us back to the
Santa María.

December 13

It is difficult to keep a journal now that we are so
busy, traveling from island to island and up and
down rivers and in and out of harbors. There are no
longer endless empty jaunts into the western sky.
But one thing has not changed. The crew continues
to grumble. They are saying this is not Asia at all,
that this whole trip has been a costly failure. They
say they will be laughed at when we finally return

home. There are no silks, no treasures, and just tiny trinkets of gold. All we will bring back are spools of rough cotton thread, a few rustic spears, and some natives who grow quieter and thinner with each day they spend on board the *Santa María*.

Columbus goes on naming everything he touches. He sees a cape of land and he says, "I christen you Cabo de la Estrella," or "Hail, Cabo del Elefante." "I name you Cabo de Cinquin," or "Isla de la Tortuga." "And you I name Puerto de San Nicolas." I am surprised he doesn't name the birds as they fly by. Every time his feet touch land he thrusts a cross into the sand and claims it for the king and queen of Spain.

The natives no longer greet us with gifts and song. Now when they see us they run. I am glad for this. Except yesterday three sailors ran after them and brought back to the ship a most beautiful young girl. Columbus wanted to talk to her and convince her that we are harmless and wish only to trade. There seemed to be an instant tenderness between her and the other native women on board, whom I've written of before. She wanted to take the women with her when she left. Columbus refused, of course, telling her to go back to her people and tell them he means no harm. The women touched hands and spoke to each other in quiet whispers. Once she was gone, the Captain turned to me and said, "Did you see the gold ring in her nose?"

The next day he sent a party to search for her and her village, and they found the village, but it had been abandoned. The fires were still warm, but not a soul was tending them. Soon they found people hiding and persuaded them to come out. They reported they even saw the beautiful girl on the shoulders of her husband. But when they returned to the ship they did not bring gold or silks. More blessed parrots.

December 16

Two nights ago we left a bay where we had been anchored. We were trying to catch the light breeze that had come up when in the moonlight we came upon a lone man in a small canoe paddling frantically in the rough water. Columbus ordered him taken aboard, and once he was with us, breathless and uncertain, he was showered with gifts. The Captain couldn't give him enough beads and bells and rings, and the man grew very happy and grateful. Columbus offered to take him to his home in our ship, which we did. The next morning we drew close to the shore and let the canoe down into the water, and the man paddled away. It wasn't long before a crowd of natives had gathered on the beach. There were hundreds of them, and they slowly paddled out to our ship, and some were taken aboard. These people were different from others we have met. They were fair, with skin as light as my own, and they brought nothing with them to trade. But when one of the crew would reach out and touch a bracelet or earring, the wearer willingly slipped it off and gave it freely. It was clear they were a gentle people. They touched our heads with two hands. And kept pointing back to shore.

There we could see a very young man arriving with much fanfare. He was clearly their king. He would not come out to us at first but stood at the shore, his arms crossed over his chest and his two old advisors close to each ear. What a sight our ship must seem to these people! The Captain sent him a gift the queen had earmarked for royalty, and he sent the message—one he now believes himself— that we are from heaven and are searching for gold. Later the young chief did come out, and Columbus treated him with great ceremony, giving him more gifts and then some food. I thought Diego would have to jump overboard to hide his laughter when

the native chief took one taste of our Castilian food and then passed it on to his advisors.

Before the chief left, he made it clear his island was ours and we had only to ask to be given whatever we need. This was much like a farmer opening the gate to let in a plague of grasshoppers. We will make the island ours. We will *take* whatever we need.

December 25

How will I ever tell my mother this? Her son has shamed her worse than any naked native or gold-greedy sailor. My friends cannot meet my eye. Ruiz scowls whenever he sees me, and even Diego pats my shoulder in pity when he passes. I hide from the Captain lest he order me tied and gagged and shot from the *Niña*'s lombard. There is nothing worse that I could possibly report. I am lucky to still have my journal. I am lucky to be alive.

Last night, after midnight, all alone and with my own two hands, I sank the *Santa María*.

It was midnight, and I turned the sandglass and called out my midnight call. I doubted that anyone heard me, though, for the crew had had a Christmas

Eve celebration at dinner. The Captain had cracked a cask of wine, and spirits had been high. No one had slept for two nights due to the natives' swarming all over the boat at unexpected hours, so the wine lulled everyone to an early sleep. Even the helmsman. I stood by him awhile, missing home and thinking of the midnight mass that my mother would go to, wrapped in her shawls against the wind from the hills. I was hoping Señor Morales had come with his wagon again this year to take her.

We were nearly ten miles east of the coast of Punta Santa, and there was no wind at all, and the sea was like a bowl of water, still and silent. Across the calm waters and under the new-moon sky, I could barely make out the mast and sails of the *Niña*.

Ruiz was at the helm, yawning and nodding. "Sancho lets me steer sometimes," I told him.

"He's not supposed to," Ruiz answered.

"But I am very good."

Need I say more? Before I knew it, Ruiz was curled at my feet, and my only concern was that the Captain would hear him snoring. I held my course, my eyes always on the right star, I swear it is so. We barely moved through the light night puffs, but soon the *Niña* seemed to drift away and I could no longer see her. I began to hear a gentle swish but took no heed of it, being tired myself, and it was all lost anyway in the squeaks and groans and rattles of the rigging. But soon there was no denying. The sound was louder, and I didn't know what it was. I was about to kick Ruiz when there was a horrible scraping and grinding, and the whole boat shuddered. I think the Captain was at the helm only seconds after Ruiz bolted to life and took the tiller from my hands. Then there was no mistaking it. I was listening to the crash of the surf on a barrier reef. And then the sound of a coral reef punching holes in our hull.

The *Santa María* is gone.

December 27

The Captain says now that it was for the best, that it was a blessing from God disguised as a catastrophe. Still, I am no longer the favored ship's boy. I have no strong voice to sing the prayers or to call the watch. I can't bear the gazes of the captured natives, and this morning I chased and swatted at a big-mouthed parrot until I pushed him right over the edge of the ship and he flew to the mast. No one can reckon with me now. Diego tries to tell me I am forgiven, that all is forgiven. But I am furious that everyone was so quick to blame me, when I did nothing wrong. I was the only one awake. I was loyal and hardworking. For this I was blamed, and forced to carry everyone else's guilt for their own drunken sleep and their cowardice.

Yes, their cowardice. The scene on the sinking ship was pathetic. When the Captain came on deck he immediately ordered an anchor to be taken to the small boat we tow astern, and the anchor to be carried far out and secured so we could pull ourselves away from the reef by pulling ourselves towards the anchor. The Captain sent Juan de la Cosa into the boat with some men, but instead of taking the anchor out, they rowed for their own lives towards the *Niña* and left us all to sink. Columbus went into a rage as they rowed away, and he ordered the *Santa María*'s heavy mainmast to be cut down to lighten her—but with each order, with each shout, we could all feel the ship grinding herself onto the sharp and deadly coral below.

Of course, the *Niña* would not take Juan de la Cosa and his men aboard but sent them back with another small boat to help. Then we were taken a group at a time to the *Niña,* where we spent the night watching the *Santa María* impale herself on the reef while the Captain wept openly in front of his men.

How grateful I am that at sunrise the native chief came aboard, and, weeping himself at our dilemma, tried to comfort Columbus with gifts of gold. With promises of more gold. And with directions to the east where gold can be found in abundance. Suddenly, upon hearing this, the Captain was saying that the *Santa María* was "too heavy and unsuitable" anyway for the business of discovery, and her sinking became—in Columbus's own words—the "predestined will of God" and a "stroke of luck."

The only luck I can imagine for myself would be to wake up in my mother's house and hear her sweeping the hearth and to know this was all a terrible dream.

January 2

Now there are forty of us crowded on board the *Niña* with twenty-two of their crew, not counting the natives the Captain has taken aboard. How strange the natives must think we are—these pale men from heaven who cram themselves in wooden tubs to float for all eternity on the sea. Even I think they are crazy—these men who are so obsessed with gold they have forgotten all about their families and their lives.

There is a solution to all this overcrowding, though. We are leaving a settlement here, on a beach within sight of the wrecked *Santa María*. The settlement's name will be La Navidad, which shames me and causes me to blush every time I hear it. The native chief has helped us salvage all we could from the wreck—wood and tools to build with, stores of food and other provisions. And the Captain has ordered the thirty-nine men who volunteered to stay to build a fortress and a tower so that Spain will have a place to come back to on future voyages. Columbus is prepared to go home to Spain now with the certainty that there is gold here, and that once a Spanish settlement has been established, our explorations will be more effective.

As I write, the lombards are shooting at the *Santa María* to sink what is left of her above the water and impress the natives with our warrior skills and our might. Me, I will be glad when I am no longer haunted by the grim stare of the broken *Santa María* off the beach. When I can leave her behind.

January 8

After some delay, we are finally under sail through the islands, following the chief's directions to gold, which we intend to check before we leave. Hours before we set sail, we heard a rumor from a native that the *Pinta*, the renegade traitor, had been seen anchored in a river. Then yesterday at noon, with a fine wind pushing us on, Columbus sent a

man up the mast to search for deep spots and shoals, but instead he spotted the *Pinta* sailing directly towards us. We were soon anchored alongside each other, and Captain Martín Alonso came aboard.

Martín Alonso was full of excuses and pardons, saying he had left Columbus against his will, but, as Diego said, the air was so thick with distrust and rage that he could have sliced it with a dagger. Martín Alonso has always been too independent and too bent on his own fame to please Columbus. And Columbus has always been too driven and powerful to give Martín Alonso any room. They bragged to each other about all the gold they had found. But the Captain made it clear he was once again in charge, and they would now return together to Spain. In his log he says he will endure this treachery in silence, glad to have a companion ship with which to make the homeward passage.

January 9

The Captain tries to favor me again, to bring me back into his circle of those who he *thinks* are his admirers and supporters. The truth is that they are all fakes and liars, smiling and bowing before him while ridiculing and criticizing him behind his back. Yesterday, to prove that all is forgiven concerning the sinking of the *Santa María*, he invited me to join him when we anchored off Monte Cristi. With a few men we rowed ashore to explore the Rio del Oro. The men had said that when they lowered their water barrels into the river here and then pulled them up, pieces of gold the size of lentils

clung to the hoops of the barrels. Columbus said he wished to see this for himself before we depart so that he could mark the spot clearly on his chart. But we saw something that to me was even more wondrous than gold.

I went along reluctantly, unwilling to grovel before the Captain, willing only to keep to my stony silence. He tried to draw me out, pointing out the large tortoises with shells like wooden shields, and then the men stopped rowing. Everyone was silent. The only motion was our silent drift and the Captain's finger tapping in the direction of three mermaids rising up out of the water. Not lovely mermaids, mind you, with flowing hair and pearls and seaweed about their slender necks, but mermaids as brawny and ugly as innkeepers' mothers, with skin as gray as slate and with grotesque webbed hands at the ends of bent arms.

"Mermaids," I whispered hoarsely to the Captain, turning in wonder to lock eyes with him.

He smiled at me and shook his head. "Manatees," he corrected. "I have seen them before, off the coast of Africa."

The men began to row again, and the manatees acted as though they hadn't seen us at all. Francisco put his back into the oars and sighed. "Reminds me of my wife," he said.

We all laughed, and the others teased him, saying, "She must be quite a cook to keep you coming back."

"And she keeps the bed warm, as well, for my icy feet."

I can't remember the last time any of us laughed. But we did today beneath the hot tropical sun, with water pouring like diamonds off the slow and steady oars. Even the Captain laughed. Even me.

January 16

We have left almost all our provisions with the men at La Navidad, planning to make some stops before heading out to sea. We've traded for fruit and breads and gathered anything else that might sustain us on the trip home. On the whole, the natives grew less and less friendly as we met them. Maybe word spread before us.

On one of the last days, some of our men went ashore and were greeted by natives with bows and arrows. These natives were different from any others they had met before. They were possibly the Caribes, who we'd been warned eat whomever they capture. They were ugly men. Their faces were smeared with charcoal, and their long hair was drawn back and gathered in clusters of parrot feathers.

Besides bows and arrows, they carried clubs.

Besides trading, they wished to capture our sailors.

At first our men were able to get them to lay down their weapons in order to trade, but soon they had taken them to hand again and came at our men with cords to tie them up. Of course, our men were

prepared at the Captain's orders, and even though there were only seven sailors and more than fifty natives, our weapons proved more powerful. They reported that one native was sliced across the buttocks, another on the chest. Our men were visibly shaken, not used to being challenged this way.

The Captain was at first troubled, and then he said, "Well, maybe this is good. They will know to be afraid of us, and if an envoy from La Navidad comes here, our people will be safe."

I don't know how safe the Captain really feels, however. Both the *Niña* and the *Pinta* are leaking terribly, and he is not willing to risk another skirmish with the natives by beaching our ships and repairing them now. So our two ships are well stocked, but leaking, as we head out at last to sea, and to Spain.

We begin a new journey in a new direction, and not counting my one disaster of judgment and inexperience, I think, to spite them all, I am becoming a seasoned sailor. I look forward to the huge swells and pulse of the open sea, where no islands beckon with false promises of gold and

treasure. I yearn for a sweep of unbroken horizon and a depth of endless fathoms. It is just the parrots and the terrible mess they make that I hate.

January 28

Table, table, sir captain and master
and good company,
Table ready; meat ready;
Water as usual for sir captain
and master and good company.
Long live the King of Castile
by land and sea!
Who says to him war, off with his head;
Who won't say amen,
gets nothing to drink.
Table is set, who don't come won't eat.

How wonderful this feels to be heading home. We almost made one extra stop. One of the natives on board told the Captain of an island on our way where only women live, where it is believed men come only part of the year and then are kicked out along with boy children who are old enough to leave their mothers. It was not the women the Captain was interested in, but the fact that this may be the island Marco Polo wrote about in his voyage to the Orient. And this would be the proof Columbus needs to show we did indeed make the Indies.

He even turned in this direction for two leagues, but when he saw how disappointed the men were—how even the thought of an island full of women did not distract them from their desire to go home, or their uneasiness about the leaking boats—he turned back towards our homeland, and now the ships roll before the winds, winds that grow cooler and cooler with each passing day.

February 2

Tonight is the night of the full moon, and once again we are traveling through a throbbing meadow of seaweed, this time at a good speed with gentle winds pushing us along. Earlier, I was not able to sleep for the eerie noise the seaweed brings, the soft, enchanted swish against the hull, like a mother's hand soothing a baby's head, so I went above and found the Captain alone on deck, lit by the moon. His log entries these last days are concerned with the miles we make and the direction we sail, constantly plotting and striving to find his way back to Spain. I was uncertain at first what to do, but finally I came up beside him. I don't think he had even looked to see who I was, when he pointed off toward the north-northeast and said, "I believe there are islands off in that quarter. When we come back on our second voyage, I will make certain we visit them."

A second voyage. Suddenly the wind was too cold for me. The moon too bright. Below, I wrap myself tight in my blanket and struggle to write. The inkhorn in one hand, the quill in the other, I try to imagine myself growing to manhood on ships such as this, and I cannot. Oh, I cannot.

February 7

For the last few days we have been sailing beneath an overcast sky at a tremendous speed, the fastest I have ever gone in my life. It nearly takes my breath away. It's growing colder, and we can no longer walk on deck without holding on. Then, yesterday, with much sadness for a few on board—myself not included—two of the parrots blew away. *Vaya con Dios.*

There is much heated discussion lately among the pilots about where we are exactly. Vicente Yáñez Pinzón says Madeira is due east. Peralonso Niño insists we will miss Madeira by thirty-eight miles. And Bartolomé Roldán says Porto Santo is due east. The Captain, probably wiser, will commit himself only to saying we are seventy-five leagues south of the parallel of Flores. What a shame the seas are too high for us to draw close to the *Pinta*. Then we could ask them what *they* think and have a few more expert opinions on where we are.

"Where are we?" they all ask. "We are right here," the ship's boy answers. And I am probably the only one who is right.

February 13

I try to write, but it is difficult. I cannot eat. I cannot bear to stand. I did not think the sea could turn on us this way. I had grown used to her gentle swells and even her strong waves and winds, but this tempest is unbearable. When I turned the sandglass tonight and feebly called out the time into the roaring storm, heavy waves of green sea and foam crashed through the rudder port, nearly drowning the helmsman and myself. Everything that was not tied down has washed overboard. Even things that were tied down have been ripped from our deck. Below, our possessions are strewn about, flying like mad birds each time we pitch and crash through this storm. The natives huddle together in terror. I cannot bear to look at their dark eyes, eyes grown huge and even *more* distrustful, if such a thing is possible.

The Captain ordered bare masts most of the night and then at sunrise put up a little sail to keep us steady. Lightning flashes, and the *Niña* labors and shudders without ceasing. The seas show no order. Huge waves come at us from opposite directions, crossing each other, breaking over our heads and crashing onto our deck. All day we are pounded and pounded. Each time a wave breaks over us, I think, *we survived that one, maybe it was the last.* But there is no end to this.

The Captain has abandoned course. The only direction he can take is to stay out from beneath the goliath waves to keep us from sinking. All night, drenched and staggering, we try to keep our light burning so the *Pinta* can keep us in sight. For a while her light flickers back. But somewhere in the night we lose her. The *Pinta* is gone.

February 14

Is it possible that things have grown worse? Nothing less than a miracle from heaven can save us now. This morning shortly after sunrise, below-decks in the dark green air of the storm, the Captain placed in a seaman's cap as many chickpeas as men in the crew. One chickpea was cut with a cross, and whoever picked that one would perform a pilgrimage once we are safely on land, a pilgrimage of gratitude to Santa María de Guadalupe in the mountains of Estremadura. The Captain himself pulled the cross on the very first draw. He swore to carry a candle weighing five pounds and to light it at the altar. Still the ocean raged.

By midday the peas were drawn again. This time it is a pilgrimage to the shrine of Santa María de Loreto in Ancona. When Pedro de Villa pulled the crossed chickpea, Columbus agreed to pay his expenses. Yet even as he spoke, a wall of water spilled down the hatchway. The ocean mocks us.

Just now a third lottery was drawn. To hold a vigil all night and have a Mass said at the church of Santa Clara de Moguer, near my home. I hoped to get this one, but the Captain picked the cross once again. Nothing matters any longer. Terrified, we have all promised to go in procession to the first shrine of the Virgin Mary if only, only we may live to see another shrine. God has forgotten us. We are so engulfed by this tempest, even He must be certain we are lost.

Later, same day

I have been hiding in the Captain's cabin, trembling from cold and fear. I am only a ship's boy. Everything is drenched with salt water except this journal and the Captain's log, which we keep wrapped together high on a shuttered shelf. It is growing dark again, and the Captain's lantern flickers and sways from the ceiling as he writes. He tells me we are sure to go down. The *Niña* will not make it, and he is furious that the *Pinta* may return and get the credit, that Martín Alonso will be the returning hero and claim all the rewards for himself. "My sons will be left orphaned and penniless," he says, "unless I can get a message to the king." So he writes his final proclamation, quickly giving accounts of the voyage and his discoveries.

He tells me, "We will wrap my proclamation in a

waxed cloth, seal it in a wooden barrel, and cast it into the sea. If we don't return, may the truth return without us." And then he turned to me and offered to include my letters in the barrel.

I hold you in my hands. You are still dry, so before you are sodden and your ink smudged, and before I change my mind, I will hand you over to my Captain. Go with God. Tell God where I am. And if you should ever reach my home, tell my mother I died with her love in my heart, and that she should pray for my foolish soul.

Go with God. And please, tell Him where I am.

Here the journal of young Pedro de Salcedo ends.

We do know from historians and scholars that, despite their fears, the *Niña* and the *Pinta* did find their way back through more storms, squalls, and rolling seas and were reunited in the harbor of Palos from which they had departed seven-and-a-half months before.

And from Francisco de Juelva (who returned from the New World with the crew of the *Pinta*, and who with his earnings bought a fishing boat), we hear that the last time Pedro de Salcedo was seen he was heading up into the hills toward his mother's house. His back was to the great ocean sea, and the ground was firm beneath his feet. Francisco said that Pedro never even looked back at the blue horizon that beckons young men to nautical adventures, and that no one really expected that Pedro de Salcedo would ever go to sea again.

AUTHOR'S NOTE

The publication of this book will happen nearly 500 years after the actual events occurred. During that time the experts on Columbus have abounded and overrun the round world. Since no one is left who was actually there, most of their knowledge is based on speculation, conjecture, theory, and wild guesses. Being a fiction writer, or a writer of "non-truths," perhaps mine are the wildest guesses of all.

But I did feel a responsibility to base my guesses on what truths I could find, and since I am not a historian, and can't translate a single word of what are believed to be the authentic logs, I found myself drawn to two experts: Robert H. Fuson, who wrote *The Log of Christopher Columbus,* and my very favorite—a man who must have been a wonderful sailing companion— Samuel Eliot Morison, who wrote *Admiral of the Ocean Sea: A Life of Christopher Columbus.*

I must also make the admission that I am a storyteller, and I had no intention of teaching you anything. To be totally truthful, I had forgotten you were there. My "soul" purpose here has been to sail through a brief period of history inside the mind and heart of a young boy, one Pedro de Salcedo. If in reading this novel you learn something, that's fine; I certainly did. But if all that happens is that you peer over the gunwale of the *Santa María* to watch the *Niña* and the *Pinta,* or you see the friendly grin of Diego or feel the ship toss and groan in its final sail, then you and I have shared a most indefinable experience.

P.C.

Pam Conrad has written many outstanding novels for young people, including *Stonewords* and *Prairie Songs*, which won the 1986 International Reading Association's Children's Book Award. She lives with her daughter in Rockville Centre, New York.

Peter Koeppen is the illustrator of *A Swinger of Birches: Poems of Robert Frost for Young People,* which became an American Book Awards Nominee. He lives in Annapolis, Maryland.